GABBY'S GOT GAME

Jenna M. Giacone

Archway Publishing books may be ordered through booksellers or by contacting:

Archway Publishing
1663 Liberty Drive
Bloomington, IN 47403
www.archwaypublishing.com
844-669-3957

Because of the dynamic nature of the Internet, any web addresses or links contained in this book may have changed since publication and may no longer be valid. The views expressed in this work are solely those of the author and do not necessarily reflect the views of the publisher, and the publisher hereby disclaims any responsibility for them.

Any people depicted in stock imagery provided by Getty Images are models, and such images are being used for illustrative purposes only.
Certain stock imagery © Getty Images.

ISBN: 978-1-6657-1802-8 (sc)
ISBN: 978-1-6657-1801-1 (e)

Print information available on the last page.

Archway Publishing rev. date: 01/28/2022

This book is dedicated to my family and friends, who helped me and pushed me to become the basketball player and person I am, and to all the children out there who question their dreams—do not let anything or anyone get in your way. Go for it all!

ACKNOWLEDGMENTS

Many thanks to all the supportive and inspirational people in my life—you know who you are. Special thanks to my parents for supporting me through all my crazy endeavors and for always believing in me. The biggest thanks to all my readers—always shoot for the stars!

Just as she did every single day, Gabby grabbed her ball from the garage and walked to the neighborhood park. She wanted nothing more in the world than to show off her basketball skills.

But just as she had done yesterday and all the days before, she sat alone in the corner and dribbled her ball.

She watched boy after boy miss easy shots. Gabby knew she was the best player at the park, but she stayed quiet, scared of what the boys would say or do if she tried to play with them.

So she just sat there and dribbled until dusk.

Gabby would dribble her ball home and rush through the dinner her mom made so she could go out back and finally shoot her ball. She would sneak some of her food to Rosco, the family dog, to help her get done more quickly.

All alone, with her ball and her hoop, Gabby heard one sound over and over and over again— *swish, swish, swish*. She made every shot she took.

The sound continued—*swish, swish, swish*— until the hoop faded in the darkness and Rosco was barking from the door. Even he knew it was time for Gabby to come inside.

Gabby washed up and got tucked in with Rosco on one side and her ball on the other. She thought about the day when she would be brave enough to play with the boys at the park.

"Maybe tomorrow!" she said as she dozed off.

"Today is the day!" Gabby told Rosco when she woke up. As she got dressed and laced up her shoes, Gabby was ready to attack the school day and play some ball.

She thought about it all day—in science class, during lunch, and even during recess. She really wanted to play with the boys at the park today, but would she have the courage to do it?

Gabby rushed home from school, grabbed her ball, and headed to the park. There, she sat in the corner and dribbled. She wanted to play so badly. But the words never came out, and she never took that step forward onto the court. Her fear was far too big.

Swish, swish, swish was even greater that night in her backyard. Gabby did not miss one single shot. Even Rosco was barking before dark because she was not missing!

Once again, Gabby went to sleep that night thinking about the next day. "Tomorrow is the day!" she said as she slowly fell asleep.

The next morning, as she was lacing up her shoes, Gabby decided to take her ball to school with her that day.

Once again, basketball, her one true love, was on her mind all through the school day.

The school bell rang, and Gabby went right to the park. Rosco was going to miss out on seeing his best friend today.

But there she sat in the corner, all alone, just dribbling her ball. Gabby wanted to play so badly. She dreamed of what would happen if she played. She heard the *swish, swish, swish* sound in her head. She knew she would dominate, but like all the previous days, she was far too scared.

The sound of a dog barking brought Gabby out of her daydreaming. Rosco came out of nowhere, and ran onto the court. He wasn't going to miss out on seeing his best friend after all. He knew exactly where to find her. All the boys stopped playing ball and were playing with Rosco on the court.

Then, without even hesitating, Gabby stepped out onto the court for the first time ever. She just wanted to get Rosco out of the way so the boys could play.

"Do you play ball?" one of the boys asked.

"Uh, just in my backyard," Gabby quietly replied.

"OK, great. We need one more player, so you're on my team," the boy said. He didn't give Gabby time to respond before tossing her his ball.

Gabby immediately started sweating. All she had ever wanted was to play somewhere other than her backyard, but she was so nervous.

Some of the boys laughed. They could not believe that their friend had just added a girl to the game.

"Oh, come on, man; girls can't hoop. She's gonna get hurt!" said one of the other boys.

But the ball was checked, and the game was on.

Gabby got the first pass and ... *swish!*

The boys looked puzzled and shocked.

After a steal, Gabby shot a far one again and ... *swish!*

"Gabby's got game!" one of the boys said.

"Quit letting her shoot; she doesn't miss!" another said.

Running back down the court, Gabby caught the ball and ... *swish!*

Over and over again—*swish, swish, swish!*

Rosco was barking from the side, and the kids watching had an echoing chant going: "Gabby! Gabby! Gabby!" All of a sudden, everyone knew who Gabby was.

She used to just be the shy girl who sat in the corner all alone, dribbling her ball.

Now, she was making some noise—*swish, swish, swish*—as more and more people came each day to watch Gabby beat the boys.

"Gabby's got game" was the cafeteria talk that week.

Strangers were talking to Gabby, and kids who used to ignore her were now sitting next to her.

Day after day at the park, the ball went *swish, swish, swish.*

She walked home each day, laughing about the fear she used to have.

She fell asleep each night with the most beautiful sound replaying over and over again: *swish, swish, swish.*

Gabby's got game.

ABOUT THE AUTHOR

Born into a sport-heavy family in Upstate New York, Jenna was introduced to basketball at a very young age. She fell in love with the sport, winning championships throughout her youth, high school, and collegiate career. A Division I basketball player and student at the University of Dayton, Jenna found the desire to write a book to share with the rest of the world. Her hope is to inspire and encourage children, especially young girls, to chase their passions and dreams no matter the obstacles or fears they may face.

CPSIA information can be obtained
at www.ICGtesting.com
Printed in the USA
BVHW021833150222
629109BV00014B/743

9 781665 718028